Where Would Santa Go?

Written by
Julia Inserro

Illustrated by
Natalie Merheb

D1404213

It was Christmas Eve. Lucy put out the cookies, along with a note she had written for Santa.

"Don't forget the carrots for the reindeer!" said her brother, Max, galloping into the room.

Dear Santa,
Please enjoy the
cookies. When i get older
i want to travel the world.
You get to see everything
on Christmas eve. Where
should i go first?
Where would you go?
Love,
Lucy and Max
and Baby Evelyn
P.S. Hugs to the
Reindeer

"Lucy...Max...wake up!" whispered Santa.

"Santa!" exclaimed Max, leaping out of bed.

"I read your note, Lucy, and thought it would be fun to show you some of my favorite places to visit. It'll be a snap in my magic sleigh, you'll see," said Santa with a smile. "I've got everything you need. Let's go!"

With just a wink from Santa, Lucy and Max found themselves flying high above the clouds.

In no time at all, they landed in a pile of snow.

"Welcome to Antarctica," said Santa. "It is one of my favorite places to come right after Christmas, because they have baby penguins! We don't have penguins at the North Pole."

"They are soooo adorable!" squealed Lucy.

"Watch me slide!" Max shouted.

Santa chuckled, "Hop back in. We have lots more to see!"

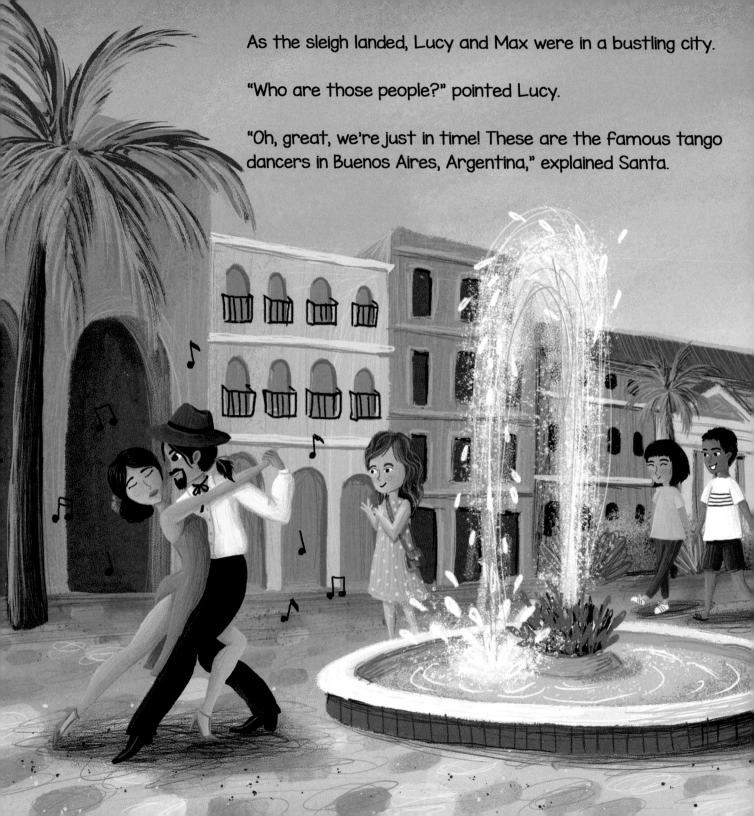

As the sleigh landed, Lucy and Max were in a bustling city.

"Who are those people?" pointed Lucy.

"Oh, great, we're just in time! These are the famous tango dancers in Buenos Aires, Argentina," explained Santa.

The rumbling of his tummy suddenly distracted Max. "What's that amazing smell?" he asked.

"Ahhh," sniffed Santa. "Those are *empanadas*. It's a delicious pastry. Let's buy some from a street cart before we head out."

"Welcome to Costa Rica!" announced Santa. "I love to hike through the rainforest. You can see lizards, ocelots and even hairy sloths here."

"I always make sure to go scuba diving with the whale sharks, too. Did you know they are the largest fish in the world and are known as gentle giants?" laughed Santa.

Max and Lucy giggled, as they hopped in the sleigh and headed off again.

"Wow!" yelled Max, pointing. "Check out those huge balloons!"

Santa maneuvered his sleigh through hundreds of brightly colored hot-air balloons.

"There are so many of them!" exclaimed Lucy.

"This is New Mexico, in the United States. If you come in October, you can see the biggest hot-air balloon festival in the world," said Santa.

"Shouldn't it be nighttime here?" asked Lucy.

"I told you my sleigh was magic, right?" winked Santa.

A little while later, Lucy peered out. "Max, look at those lights dancing in the sky. How beautiful!"

"I thought you might like to see the Aurora Borealis, also known as the Northern Lights," grinned Santa. "Iceland is right below us and this is one of the best light shows in the world."

"It's amazing!" gushed Max. "What's next? Can we go to see some castles and dragons, or maybe a lion?"

"Hmm. Let me see what I can do," replied Santa with a big smile. "Hold on!"

"Check this out," said Santa, zipping around the mountains.

"Oh, my! It looks like a scene from a fairy tale," said Lucy.

"Yes, it does," smiled Santa. "This is Germany. It's full of amazing castles!"

"I don't see any dragons," muttered Max.

"True, but how about a giant temple and some mummies?" offered Santa.

"Woo hoo!" shouted Max. "Let's go!"

Santa parked his sleigh near a line of stone statues.

Putting some sunglasses on, Lucy said, "It sure is hot and sunny here."

"We are in Egypt now," Santa told them. "This is Karnak Temple. It is 4,000 years old."

"Are these statues supposed to be dragons?" asked Max eagerly.

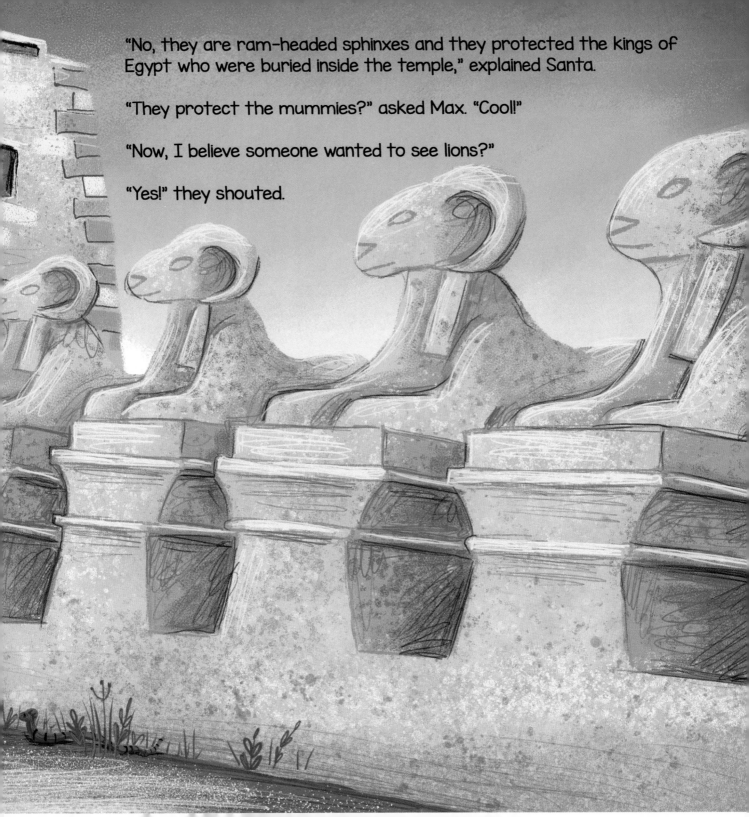

"No, they are ram-headed sphinxes and they protected the kings of Egypt who were buried inside the temple," explained Santa.

"They protect the mummies?" asked Max. "Cool!"

"Now, I believe someone wanted to see lions?"

"Yes!" they shouted.

With just a quick hop, the sleigh landed on a flat dusty plain.

"Welcome to Tanzania," announced Santa. "It has some of the world's best wildlife preserves. They protect as much land as they can for the animals, many of whom are endangered."

"Let's jump out here and get into a proper safari vehicle," Santa suggested. The open-air jeep bounced along as they headed toward a pack of sleepy lions.

"They're amazing," Max whispered.

Santa smiled. "Let's head over and see the rhinos, hippos and giraffes before we have to leave."

At their next stop, Lucy and Max found themselves in a busy open-air market. All around them, people were shouting loudly, trying to sell their wares to the shoppers walking by.

"This is Morocco!" beamed Santa. "The market, or *souk* as it's called here, in Marrakesh, is always busy. Let's walk through and find some souvenirs. But watch out for the camels - they can be a little grumpy. Then, I'm going to show you my next favorite place."

"Welcome to Oman," announced Santa, as Lucy and Max jumped out of the sleigh. "It is one of my favorite places in the Middle East. We can swim with the sea turtles or hike through the canyons, or *wadis*, to see hidden waterfalls. We can even camp in the desert!"

"We want to do it all!" yelled Lucy and Max together.

"The next spot I want to show you is Nepal. During the spring they have a festival called *Holi* where everything becomes a rainbow. They do this in India, too."

"They're throwing paint at each other!" exclaimed Lucy.

"It's a big party to celebrate the spring," replied Santa, laughing. "It's tons of fun!"

Lucy and Max looked at each other. "We want to be rainbows, too!" they shouted, dashing out of the sleigh.

After another short trip, Santa guided them down and landed near a beautiful temple. Everywhere they looked, Lucy and Max saw trees covered in pink and white flowers.

"It's beautiful!" exclaimed Lucy. "It's like a fairy village."

"Smells great, too," added Max.

"This is Japan. Every year I try to come to their spring Cherry Blossom Festival, since we don't have flowers at the North Pole," said Santa. "Let's go grab some cherry blossom cookies and relax under the trees before we head off again."

"I think our last stop for tonight will be New Zealand," announced Santa, as he landed the sleigh. "This is where I come when I want to go white water rafting, flying along a zipline, and bungee jumping!"

"We want to do all of that!" yelled Lucy and Max, jumping around in circles.

Laughing, Santa said, "You have a pretty long list of things you guys are going to do. Do you think you have seen enough for tonight?"

"Well, we are pretty tired, but there's one more place I would love to see before we go home," said Lucy with a smile.

Santa winked, "I think I know exactly where you want to go!"

As the sleigh descended under the bright
moonlight, Lucy and Max gazed in wonder. There
it was - Santa's village at the North Pole.

"It looks magical," whispered Lucy.
The elves and Mrs. Claus waved
as they flew past.

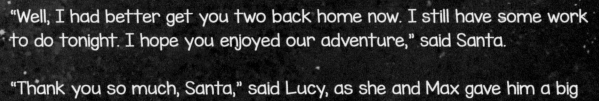

"Well, I had better get you two back home now. I still have some work to do tonight. I hope you enjoyed our adventure," said Santa.

"Thank you so much, Santa," said Lucy, as she and Max gave him a big hug. "I loved seeing all your favorite places. This has been the best Christmas ever."

On Christmas morning, Lucy and Max's mom came into their room.

"Merry Christmas, sleepyheads! Goodness gracious! Where did you get all this stuff?"

"It was amazing!" yawned Lucy. "Santa took us to his favorite places all over the world! We saw Argentina, Morocco, Japan, Nepal and even Egypt! I can't wait until Christmas Eve next year."

"Me, too," said Max sleepily. "But next time, I'm asking to see dragons first."

Go get your FREE COUNTDOWN 'TIL SANTA calendar at:

WWW.JULIAINSERRO.COM

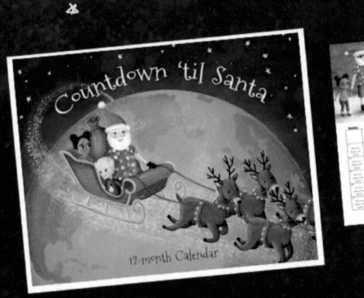

And check out these other books by Julia Inserro:

Dedicated to my three magic beans, L, M & N – who just can't get enough of Santa – and all the other TCK kids who explore the world and can find adventure in every corner.

– J.I.

To Mom and Dad – thanks for all your love and support.

–N.M.

For freebies and updates on new releases, subscribe at www.juliainserro.com.

Author: Julia Inserro (www.juliainserro.com)
Illustrator: Natalie Merheb (www.nataliemerheb.com)

Printed in the United States of America

First Printing, 2019

ISBN 978-1-947891-03-6